This book belongs to:

_____

This paperback edition first published in Great Britain in 2017
by Andersen Press Ltd., 20 Vauxhall Bridge Road, London SW1V 2SA.
First published in Great Britain in 2016 by Andersen Press Ltd.,
Copyright © Michael Foreman, 2016.
The rights of Michael Foreman to be identified as the author and illustrator
of this work have been asserted by him in accordance with the
Copyright, Designs and Patents Act, 1988.
All rights reserved.
Colour separated in Switzerland by Photolitho AG, Zürich.
Printed and bound in Malaysia.
10 9 8 7 6 5 4 3 2 1
British Library Cataloguing in Publication Data available.
ISBN 978 1 78344 499 1

TUFTY

The Little Lost Duck who Found Love

Michael Foreman

ANDERSEN PRESS

A family of ducks lived on an island in the middle of a lake.
At the edge of the lake there was a beautiful palace and a park.
Each morning the ducklings paddled along behind their mother.
The youngest, Tufty, always struggled to keep up.

"The Royal Duck and Duckess are very kind," Mother Duck told her children. "They always give us breakfast. See how they walk like us with their wings folded behind them."

Some evenings, Tufty and the other ducks
watched the Duck and Duckess dance at
grand parties under great crystal chandeliers.

As the golden summer passed, the nights grew colder and the ducklings cuddled closer.

"Soon, we will have to fly south where the winter is warmer," said Father Duck, "so practise your flying, little ducks."

One day, Father Duck said, "Time to go!" And off they flew,
up and away from the lake, and the palace and park.

Tufty was amazed to see that all around the park was a huge city. Roads and railways criss-crossed between towering buildings that seemed to touch the cloudy sky.

Poor Tufty struggled to keep up with the other ducks. The tall buildings made it even more difficult and soon he lost sight of his family.

He flew on, growing more tired and lost. Then it began to rain and get dark. "I must find a safe place to rest," he thought. Suddenly he saw what looked like an island amongst the traffic.

Tufty landed safely, but the
noise of the roaring traffic
all around was frightening.
Exhausted, he took shelter
in a tunnel leading down
under the island.

A man was sitting in the quiet tunnel. "Hello, little one," he said. "This isn't a good place for a duck. Here, have something to eat, then we will find a better place for you."

The man shared his food with Tufty and then scooped him up into his arms. "Let's go, little one."

They left the
thundering traffic
behind them and came
to a dark wood next to a
small lake. The man moved
some branches from the foot of
a chestnut tree. "Welcome to my
home, little one," he said.

Tufty saw that the tree was
hollow, and inside was dry
with a bed of straw.
Feeling tired but safe he
fell asleep in the man's hat.

Tufty woke to the wonderful smell of cooking. Pigeons cooed in the tree and a family of squirrels waited for a share of the man's breakfast. The quiet lake was covered in mist.

After breakfast Tufty got ready for the lonely flight south. But the mist still hid the tops of the trees and Tufty knew he would never find his way on his own.

So he spent the winter sleeping in the man's hat, sharing his meals and slowly growing bigger and stronger.

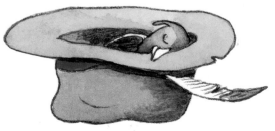

In the springtime, as the days grew warmer, Tufty saw
flocks of ducks flying overhead. His family was returning
to the lake beside the palace. Tufty flew up to join them.

Together they flew back to the palace gardens.
Each day, more and more ducks arrived at the lake.

Tufty noticed a little brown duck. He thought
he had never seen anyone more beautiful.
"Let's get away from the crowd," he said to her
one day. "Let's spread our wings and fly away."

Together, they flew to the lake in the woods.
Trees were bursting into blossom and the chestnut
tree was more beautiful than any chandelier.

"Just in time for tea," smiled the man.
"Welcome home."